Forgiven by Love

By
Ruth Bawell

Table of Contents

Unsolicited Testimonials

By **Phyllis**

⭐⭐⭐⭐⭐ **Love Ruth!**

I love Ruth's books! Her mysteries are the best!

⭐⭐⭐⭐⭐ **Love This Author**

Ruth Bawell is very creative and a great writer! All her books have left me unable to stop reading till the ending! There were a few Amish fact mistakes, like unmarried man having a beard, but the plot was so good I overlooked that!

By **Steve M**

⭐⭐⭐⭐⭐ **I love romance stories** August 5, 2017
I love romance stories... well written with her usual twists to the story still enjoyed them very much Once I start I can't put it down.

By **Bones**

⭐⭐⭐⭐⭐ **Amish County Stories**
I love all the Amish County stories! Each one brings so much excitement! Ruth Bawell is also a wonderful writer!

By **Kindle Customer**

⭐⭐⭐⭐⭐ **Good clean writing.**
The Amish stories of Ruth Bawell are authentic, faith-filled writings. They are short, more the length of novellas or longer short stories. Always clean, always uplifting.

FREE GIFT

Just to say thanks for checking our works we like to gift you

Our Exclusive Never Before Released Books

100% FREE!

Please GO TO

http://cleanromancepublishing.com/gift

And get your FREE gift

Thanks for being such a wonderful client.

Chapter One

It was a nicely cool September morning. Hannah arrived at the bakery quite early, around six a.m., to start setting up the ingredients for the day's menu. First, she changed into her working dress, put on a pair of black boots, and stepped out to the back of the bakery to bring in some of the charcoal stored in the warehouse. She got a supply of them every weekend to use in the local oven for baking. She grabbed a bag of charcoal and carried it into the rusty wheelbarrow that stood by the wall. Then she pushed it into the oven site.

Hannah picked a box of matches from the tabletop and started to make the fire. Next, she washed her hand thoroughly in a bucket of water reserved for hand washing at the bakery and wiped them meticulously with a towel. Her long brunette hair was neatly braided and wrapped in a bun on the back of her head. Finally, she gently adjusted her covering and bonnet and put on her kitchen apron.

After Hannah had readied the kitchen area, she reached for the bags of groceries she had picked from the grocery store the day before, unpacked them on the worktable, and sorted them out. She brought out storage bags and containers, emptying each content into their respective space.

She had spent the night before putting together a prep list. She knew by heart what the villagers loved to buy from the store. She had worked at this bakery since she was a child, with her parents as the owners then, of course. After they passed, they had willed it to her, and she had somehow found a way to manage it successfully, having had full firsthand experience and tutelage from them.

Now, batches of breakfast pastries, shoofly pies, whoopie pies, puddings, cookies, muffins, and sweet cakes had to be made and ready before the bakery doors opened up for the day. Hannah measured cups of baking flour into a big round bowl placed on the table. She measured baking powder and baking soda, a teaspoon of salt, and other ingredients into the bowl. She melted some butter, added sugar, and began to whisk it thoroughly with a spatula.

After getting the right texture, Hannah poured the dry mix into the bowl and whisked some more. Next, she broke some eggs into another bowl and slowly began mixing them into the batter. This, she made for the cakes. And then, in another bowl, she began mixing more batches of flour for the pastries.

Hannah then began to prepare the fruit and sweet cream fillings for the pastries and cakes. Her younger sister, Becca, who helped out at the bakery, had taken the day off, so she had her hands full with work.

Hannah sighed, feeling tired already. At twenty-four, Hannah had experienced life in all its throes. She had married at nineteen and had her boy, Jeremiah, aged five, and his brother, Noah, some two years later. When her husband, Elijah, died, it was a shock to all of them.

But it was not the first shock of heartbreak Hannah had felt.

Like it so often did, Hannah felt her memories taking her back in time…

Hannah was sixteen when she met Amos. He was eighteen years at the time. The two had met at a Sing, and they had both become quite enamored. Hannah was hoping Amos would ask her to court soon.

One Sunday evening, Hannah had gone to the Sing to meet with Amos, but he never showed up. She searched for him among the young men seated before them in rows, but he was nowhere to be found. While the merriments and games took place, she waited with fading hopes, watching as the couples started to say their goodbyes, leaving in pairs. Finally, as the congregation began to lessen, she caught sight of his cousin, Nathaniel holding hands with Mary, one of Hannah's closest friends to whom he was engaged.

Hannah had waved and ran up to them to find out what could have been the problem.

"Hey! Have you two seen Amos today? He didn't show up to pick me up as he promised, so I had to ride with my brothers. I have been so worried, because that's so unusual of him," she inquired as she hugged Mary.

"He didn't tell you?" Nathaniel asked.

"Tell me what?" she responded with anxious concern.

Nathaniel stared at her, expressionless. She was losing her patience. She looked from Nathaniel to Mary and back again, searching their expressions for clues.

"What are you talking about, Nat? What is wrong with Amos?"

That was when Nathaniel realized that she genuinely had no idea about what had happened earlier in the day. He excused Mary and pulled Hannah away from the small crowd of boys and girls still dancing and chatting cheerfully to a quieter place, where he sat her down.

Hannah couldn't help but feel apprehensive.

Did Amos get into an accident? Had he found some other girl and decided to stop seeing her but couldn't find the courage to break things off in person? What was going on?

Nath paced around for a moment, then he held her by the shoulders. She was shaking as her heart was beating out of her chest.

"Amos left," he finally blurted out.

"Left?" retorted Hannah. "What do you mean left?" she demanded, her voice straining with confusion.

"Amos left town. He's been contemplating that for a while now. The opportunity came some days back when we visited the farmer's market last weekend to trade our newly handcrafted woodwork. Amos found out there was a bus that would be departing this morning and so he decided to join them. You know Amos, he has eyes for the large cities, the tourists, the cars. But don't worry," Nathaniel explained calmly. "He's not leaving the faith, just moving to a different community. One with more... opportunities."

By now, hot tears were streaming down Hannah's cheeks, and she couldn't control them, nor did she even care to wipe them clean.

"How long?" she questioned.

"What?" Nathaniel asked.

"How long ago has he been planning this move?"

"Since we were kids. Amos has always had this dream. He used to talk about it so much since we were like eight years old, Hannah. He wants to share his woodwork with more people, and has never been as bothered by the Englisher tourists as some other folks."

"So how come he didn't tell me? How come it never came up in any of our conversations? He had just asked me to court him. Did that mean nothing?" Hannah queried. She was feeling enraged and helpless at the same time. Finally, she dropped her head and began to cry.

Nathaniel stood there, not knowing what to do. When she was spent and had wiped her eyes with the hem of her skirt, he placed one hand on her shoulder. "Look, for what it's worth, you're the only girl my cousin has ever been in love with. He has never spoken of any girl the way he does you. I'm guessing he was too afraid to tell you himself. I bet he's full of regrets as we speak."

Hannah looked up at him squarely and retorted. "No, he didn't love me. He never cared about me, lest he'd never leave me alone and heartbroken, or he would have at least had the decency to tell me by himself and break things off."

"I'm sorry, Hannah. I'm sorry," Nathaniel managed, lost for words.

"Don't be, but thank you for telling me. At least now I know what a coward he was." Then, with tear-clouded eyes, she turned around and ran back home, anguished, wondering what she may have done to not deserve an explanation or goodbye from him.

Months passed by, and although Hannah held hopes that one day, she'd open her front door and find Amos standing outside with one knee on the ground, begging her to forgive and take him back, it never happened.

Not a letter. Not a card. And even when Nathaniel married her friend, Mary, some months afterward, Amos never showed up. No one heard of him or from him.

Finally, Hannah decided that it was time to move on. He didn't care for her as much as she did for him. Hence she needed to move on from him. So she devoted herself to work in the bakery to help get her mind off him in those excruciating months after his departure. And when it was clear that he wasn't coming back, Hannah swore to herself never to have anything to do with him ever again.

***

For the next year, Hannah refused to accept invitations to the Sing from the boys in the village. Her parents had even tried to matchmake her on a few occasions with some of the suitable boys in the village, but Hannah would not budge. She had somehow convinced herself that she was never going to love anyone ever again. She would not risk her heart; instead, she would live out the rest of her life alone, pouring herself into her work and expanding the bakery as much as possible.

One evening, after the family was done eating dinner and had finished their chores, Hannah's mother called her out to the porch. They both sat on the swing bench on the veranda.

"Hannah dear," her mother began. "I understand that you've been hurt by that boy, but Hannah, you can't just give up on ever marrying because of that. So much time has passed by. You'll have to let go of the past and find some boy to court. There are a lot of good boys around here who would make a good husband for you. Please, consider one of them," she said while reaching for her hand.

"But mama," Hannah protested, "how can I ever love again? It still hurts so badly, and every time I even consider another boy, it feels like they're all going to be the same way. They'll leave me eventually," she sobbed.

"No, dear. No, they won't!" her mother comforted her.

"How do you know that, *mamm*? How can you be so sure?" Hannah questioned.

"Well, there's only one way to find out, isn't it? Your father and I will put our eyes out for a worthy young man for you, or we can ask your brothers to recommend one of their friends if you approve. How does that sound?"

"Okay, mother. I'll think about it," she replied as her mother wiped her face clean with her blouse. The two women locked themselves in each other's embrace for a minute.

Hannah's mother finally patted her on her back.

"Now go inside and get some sleep, daughter. We have a big day tomorrow at the farmer's market."

Chapter Two

Hannah, Becca, and their mother woke up at the break of dawn to prepare breakfast for the family. They also baked varieties of pastries to be sold to the uptown farmers who would come around to buy their products in bulk and the tourists who enjoyed visiting their community to get a glimpse of what life was for them. The tourists chatted excitedly like schoolchildren on an excursion and spoke in funny accents. They always had cameras out, taking photos of animals, food, fruits, and woodworks.

Her father and four brothers were already milking the cows and hanging up fresh fodder for their afternoon meal, stacking the carriage with produce from last evening's harvest. Baskets of tomatoes, corn, potatoes, and green beans were loaded up, and piles of fodder for the livestock were neatly bundled up in the back.

Soon they were set to leave for the farmer's market. Her mother had carefully placed the pastries into another basket. The boys rode on a different carriage while her father rode the ladies in another buggy. The metal wheels of the horse-drawn carriages screeched and creaked as they rode along the steeped village roads, occasionally meeting and exchanging greetings with other farmers and neighbors who were also on their way to the farmer's market.

The early morning sun was just clearing up as they arrived at the market. The men and women quickly offloaded the fruits, vegetables, food crops, and baked goodies onto the produce booths. Traditional items and pieces of furniture made by woodworkers were arranged on ledges. Homemade pork, turkey sausage, oven-roasted turkey breasts sliced thin for lunch meat, and hand-rolled soft pretzels were beautifully arranged across tables in glass wares on each stand. Young girls waited on customers at the booths as they started to arrive.

Hannah had left Becca and her mom at the stand to meet with Mary, her friend. Mary was carrying a slightly visible bump and had come to the market with her husband, Nathaniel, to trade his handcrafted woodwork. They had moved to live near Nathaniel's mother, who had a farm about forty minutes away.

"Hello, Mary," Hannah called out, waving.

"Hannah," Mary screamed delightedly as she turned around to see her friend. The two girls squealed and jumped into each other's arms.

"Mary, I've missed you so much," Hannah said and, on sighting the bump, added, "Well, guess who's baking a little bun in the oven."

Mary giggled and twirled around.

"I'm so happy for you, Mary. How is Nat?"

"He's fine. He's over there stacking the artworks on the shelves. So, tell me, how has life been with you? Are you seeing someone now?"

Hannah shrugged as they sat on the wooden bench in front of the booth.

"There's not much to tell. My life is very uninteresting, and I'll probably grow old single and alone," she joked.

"Don't say that," Mary chastised, with a serious look on her face. "Don't ever say that. There are lots of fine young men in town and beyond for you. You just have to make a choice."

The two women conversed at length before Hannah excused herself to return to their booth.

"Take care of yourself, dear Mary," she said as they warmly embraced each other.

"You too, Hannah, and don't forget what I've said, alright?"

Hannah let out a laugh. "I won't," she replied with a grin.

Mary held her hand. "Promise?"

"I promise," Hannah replied with all sincerity.

"Hello, Hannah," a male voice called out from behind as she hurried back to her booth. The voice was vaguely familiar, and she wished for a second it was who she thought it was. When she turned around, she met Elijah Wood standing behind her, holding his horse's harness in hand.

"Oh," Hannah flustered. "Hello, Elijah." She shot him a disappointed glance.

Elijah nodded understandingly.

"Were you expecting someone else?" he asked, embarrassed.

"No--no. Not at all," Hannah stammered, feeling ashamed of herself for behaving in such an unkind manner. Finally, she muttered a barely audible apology under her breath.

"It's alright. Hannah, can we maybe talk? Later? You seem to be in a hurry. I... I-- would like us to have a chat when you're less engaged," Elijah managed.

"Okay. I'll come meet you at your shed," Hannah answered curtly and waved him goodbye.

When Hannah walked into their stall, her mother and sister were eagerly awaiting her.

"Hannah. Who was that I saw you talking to?" her mother queried.

"Stop it, mama. He didn't even say anything yet. He wants us to meet later. That is all. We are just friends."

Hannah shook her head and sighed as she moved on to speak to a customer who had just shown up at their booth.

Later that evening, Hannah met with Elijah. After much small talk, he finally asked Hannah to the Sunday evening hymn sings, offering her a ride to and from the church in his buggy. Hannah asked for some time to consider his proposal.

Elijah Wood was the sixth son of Adam Woods. Theirs was a large family of seven boys and two girls. At twenty, he was too tall and too lanky for his age, with tiny freckles on his face. He looked quite timid and would often stammer when speaking with someone he'd just met. He wasn't quite the catch, and many of the girls in the community had turned down courting with him. However, he bore a hidden crush on Hannah from the time they had started the first grade together in their one-room classroom in the community.

$$***$$

As dusk gathered on Sunday evening the next week, Elijah got into his single-bench seat buggy piloted by his horse and set out on the road to Hannah's house. Together, they drove to church to participate in the group singing with other youths that had come, many seeking a date with potential spouses.

After the singing sessions, the two returned to Hannah's home, where they were served dinner, and Elijah got to spend time with the family. When dinner was done, the couple spent the rest of the evening together playing board games on the floor with her siblings.

One by one, the other children retired to bed while the two remained. They talked quietly until Hannah's father said it was time for the evening to end. Hannah stood on the porch and waved Elijah goodbye as Elijah got into his buggy and rode back home.

Elijah and Hannah began courting officially some two weeks later. Hannah realized that he was much more than he appeared to be. He was intelligent and well-versed, as well as kind and loving. The more time they spent together, the more similarities they discovered about each other. A close bond was soon formed, and the two fell deeply in love.

"You know, I realize how little I really knew about you," Hannah said one day. They were on a buggy ride to the river, where some other people their age were meeting for a picnic on one of the last warm days of the season.

"Well, a lot of people think so, and they still do. I guess it's because I'm pretty quiet. People tend to judge a book by its cover, you know. But still, it took a lot of courage to ask you out," Elijah admitted.

"So, tell me, what made you decide to approach me?" Hannah asked.

Elijah looked her in the eye and sighed. "I have always cared deeply for you but did not realize it. But when I found out you and Amos were together, I knew it then. I thought I had lost you, and I felt such a sadness. Like my heart was broken, although I wanted you to be happy."

Hannah paused for a while and sighed before saying, "Okay, so after Amos left, why didn't you express interest?"

"Well, I didn't think you were ready. You needed your space to heal, and I respected that. So I came when I felt it was the right time."

"And now, here we are. Perhaps we were destined to be, and I'm glad you came into my life."

"So am I," Elijah agreed as they reached for each other's hands across the buggy seat.

Hannah enjoyed spending time together with Elijah. She couldn't believe her luck. Elijah was a kind man, diligent and hardworking. He would always offer support at the bakery whenever he had time.

During the planting season, when her father was too sick to work the farms, Elijah joined her brothers, and together, they plowed the fields and planted the seeds. He continued to care for the field until her father was back on his feet, strong enough to go back into the fields. And when her father relapsed again a few months later and passed, he was there for Hannah through the grieving period. He proved to be a strong support system for her and her family.

In their spare time, the two would go on long rides, exploring the small roads around the community and talking of their plans for the future.

Finally, he had asked her to marry him. Hannah still had the lovely porcelain dish he had gifted her with on that day. It had belonged to his grandmother, and hers before that.

Chapter Three

By fall the next year, after the harvest season, the two were married in a traditional ceremony held at Hannah's family house. Hannah was adorned in her newly sewn navy-blue dress, which she had made all by herself. Elijah was dressed in a black suit, coat, and hook-fastened vest, standing before their many guests to share their vows.

After the wedding, the new couple remained in Hannah's parents' home. They were given a bedroom in the house richly decorated with handcrafted woodwork furnishings, where they lived for the next six months, spending their time visiting relatives and friends, working together at the bakery and in the barnyard before they finally moved out to start their own family.

Soon, Hannah was pregnant with their first. By now, Elijah, with the combined help of their family members and friends, had built them a home close to their parents' home and cultivated a farm. He had also built a barn adjoining their house where they planted food crops and vegetables all year round.

Hannah continued to support her mother at the bakery and would often help out in the farm work and at the barn. During harvests, Elijah would transport their surplus food crops into the town for sale in the farmer's market. Hannah would accompany him, but with her advancing pregnancy, she was advised to stay home.

Occasionally, Elijah would join a group of farmers on a trip to visit other farms and learn new acceptable strategies for more sufficient crop yield and management of the animals, especially with the recent outbreak of diseases that fatally affected their horses.

It was on one of such excursions, a year after their second son, Noah, was born, that Elijah had embarked on another journey with some local farmers when an unfortunate tragedy occurred. By the following evening, they were to return, but no news was heard from them. Anxious and filled with dread at such an unusual development, Hannah and a few women quickly asked for help from the elderly male community members.

The men had swung into action, and words were sent out. It was later that night that news got to the county that the bus transporting Elijah and the other farmers had been rear-ended by a reckless truck driver who was speeding against traffic regulations.

Elijah and two others were among the fatalities.

***

The diner bell dinged, snapping Hannah out of her reminisce. She looked up as the diner doors pushed open, and a man dressed in black pants and a shirt with suspenders waddled in. It was Herr Samuel, the farmer who delivered fresh cow milk to the bakery every morning.

"Guten Morgen, Herr Samuel," Hannah greeted while rushing out from behind the counter to collect the delivery from him.

"Morgen, Hannah. How are you today?"

"I'm quite good. It's a lovely morning. Thank you for the milk," she said as she set the keg on the table.

"How are you feeling today?"

The old man grunted, heaving himself into one of the seats behind him

"Like a very old man," he said and chuckled.

Hannah smiled. "How about a cup of tea and pie?"

"Ah! That would be nice. Thank you."

Hannah went behind the counter to fix him a cup.

"How are Becca and the boys?" Mr. Samuel called out after she had left.

"They're doing great. Becca took the day off and is home with Noah, who is a bit ill today."

"That's a shame. I hope the boy feels better soon."

Hannah nodded, then turned as the bell dinged again. A woman and her two teenage girls in plain, blue-colored dresses and white and black bonnets walked in. Hannah set Mr. Samuel's pie on the table and turned away to attend to the customers, all thoughts of the past gratefully pushed from her mind for now.

Chapter Four

It was one of the big farmer's market days. The smell of freshly picked fruits and vegetables filled the air. There were hums of voices and smiling faces at each stand.

Freshly baked goodies like shoofly pie, sticky buns, cookies, apple dumplings, muffins, and cakes filled the tables. Sellers and buyers were bargaining and trading goods and services.

Nathaniel sat in front of his stall, gazing into the midday sunlight as if he were anticipating someone.

The atmosphere was filled with blissful chatty bustles. Men discussed in hushed tones. Women chatted and haggled in high-pitched voices. Children laughed and played cheerfully, scrambling from stall to stall, and girls stood before their displays as they gossiped about the boys who were also in trios or groups discussing them. The horses brayed and whinnied as they chewed on fresh fodder hanging from the shacks.

Nathaniel had come to the market with his children as they often did. His wife and twin daughters were a few stands away bargaining with some English shoppers who were picking fresh apples and potatoes off the tables into their sorting baskets.

He looked up to see a man who looked familiar walking down the aisle between the stalls. The man stopped at one of the first woodwork stalls and spoke to the storekeeper. Nathaniel kept looking closely at the man as he gestured as if he was describing an individual. They communicated for a few minutes before the storekeeper turned and pointed in Nathaniel's direction.

The man began to walk towards his stall, and the closer he came, the clearer his features were. Although it had been over ten years since he last saw him, Nathaniel could tell who it was.

"Amos!" Nathaniel gasped.

Amos was Nathaniel's cousin, the son of his father's younger sister. The two had grown up together as children under the same roof.

Amos's parents had died when he was still very young, and Nathaniel's father had adopted him into the family and raised him as he would a son. As Nathaniel was the only biological son of his father, the two grew a strong bond, and they were more brothers than cousins. And as they grew into maturity, they both worked at Nathaniel's father's shop, learning to turn raw lumber into handcrafted furnishings. They worked together on big projects but were permitted to keep the money from small objects they made on their own.

As the boys turned seventeen, Amos had begun to hint that he was dissatisfied with the monotonous life of their community. He wanted to move to live with his other cousin, who had a farm in a community near a sizeable Englisher town. It would be a chance for him to have a larger market for his wooden crafts, and he could save faster for a home of his own.

Even though he had begun courting Hannah, whom he was very much in love with, he knew he could not stay. He was sure he would come back soon, but this was his chance to earn—and be celebrated for his craft at the same time.

When it was clear that his mind was made up, his father blessed him and let go, telling him to come home anytime.

And it seemed, now was finally the time.

The two men were all smiles as they rushed into each other's embrace.

"Amos, is this you?" Nath exclaimed.

"Yes, brother. It's been ages. I'm so happy to see you, Nath."

"Same, Same. This is good. This is the Lord's doing."

"Right," Amos chuckled as they shook hands again

"Come, meet my wife. You know Mary, of course. We got married after you left town. And we have four lovely children. Come, come say hi to them."

The two men moved to the stall where Nathaniel's family stood. Mary stood up as they approached.

"Mary dear, you remember Amos, don't you?" Nathaniel said.

"Of course," Mary said. Their twin daughters also said greetings.

"Where are the boys?" Amos asked.

"Oh! They're on the other side of the market trading their handcrafted woodwork," Nathaniel responded, pointing to the area where the boys were.

"Just like the two of us, huh, when we were young boys," Amos said thoughtfully, and the two men laughed.

As he turned around and observed the market, he whispered, "Not much has changed around here, brother. It still feels and smells the same way it did when we used to run around from stall to stall, trying to trade off our woodwork for a few dimes."

His friend smiled. "Come, let's sit awhile. We will be heading home soon," Nathanial said.

The two men walked back to the woodworking stand. Amos picked up a figurine from the table and turned it around in his fingers.

"It feels so good to be home. If you need help with work, I can assist. I never stopped woodworking, you know. That's how I made life over there, and I had the opportunity to learn a lot. There are a few new handy skills I picked up, which I will show you."

"Well, woodworking skill is in the family," Nathanial laughed. "I've got two big projects at hand. With you around now, it means less time spent on one job. You will be quite helpful."

"How is Father?" Amos asked as he took a seat on one of the newly crafted wooden stools.

"He's all right. Old, but strong-willed. Father has always held on to hope that you'd come back someday. I'm glad he's still alive to see today. He will be very pleased to see you. I feel he's been holding on for this day, for you."

Amos felt a whirlwind of emotions.

"I miss him so much. Going away was good for me in many ways, but I don't feel like it was worth all the things I missed out on. It took me two years to finally decide to come back home. I feel like perhaps I let many people down."

"You did right, Amos. I feel it's a good thing that you got to experience what you had always yearned for. I mean, imagine that you had spent all your life here without finding out for yourself what it's worth. I bet you would feel a lot more miserable than you do now. You made the call. You have to make peace with your choices and move on, because now that you're back, a whole future lies ahead for you to explore." Nathaniel spoke gently, trying to ease him out of his guilty state of mind.

With a sigh, Amos finally agreed. "I guess you're right," he said, nodding his head as he considered his friend's words.

The two men kept talking about all they'd missed in each other's life until the sun began to set. Then, they packed their unsold produce into the buggy and all headed to Nathanial's house.

Amos went in to see his father when they arrived at the family house. Although the old man was displeased he had wandered for much longer than expected, he was happy to have him back home in the fold.

Later that night, after the family had gone to bed, Nathaniel came out to find Amos sitting outside with his fist under his chin.

"Here's the prodigal son I've been looking for all around the house," Nathaniel teased as Amos stood on the porch in a pensive mood. "Any problem?" he asked.

Amos stood up, heaved a deep sigh, and hesitated.

"Is Hannah still in town? How is she? Did she find someone? I never quit thinking of her, you know. I should-- I should never have left."

"You still love her, don't you?" Nathaniel inquired, gazing over at his shadow emanating from the local lantern hung on the porch roof, then he continued. "She got married about three years after you left. Amos, Hannah waited for you. Even though she was so mad at you for leaving, and we were all sad and disappointed, she waited until she lost hope. Then she found someone and got married. I'm sure you remember Elijah, one of the Wood boys. They have two boys."

Nathaniel sadly explained Elijah's untimely demise. Amos was lost for words. Then, after a while, he sighed.

"It must have been so tough on her," he surmised.

"It was. So, you have to tread carefully and best to avoid her if you'll bring nothing but chaos into her life again. You hurt her once. It would be cruel to hurt her again."

Amos considered all that Nathaniel had said that night, which left him very regretful. He decided that he was going to be a man. He would make it up to Hannah. He was going to redeem himself, not just before Hannah, but Nathaniel and everyone else, but most importantly, for Hannah and her boys.

He could be a father figure in their lives, just like his uncle had stood up and raised him when his father had died. He was going to win Hannah back.

Chapter Five

The barn needs fixing.

Hannah sighed as she closely inspected the part of the wooden fence facing the path where the horses roamed during the day. The wood had worn out due to the heavy downpour from the last season and was wide enough for a horse or two to break through.

She had spent the evening cleaning out the stables, changing the water, and hanging up dry hay and leftover apples in a feeding bucket for the horses to munch on during the night. She casually reached out and caressed one of the horse's manes. The animal whinnied and leaned towards her, dipping its mouth into her palm. She smiled warmly and patted it, as she remembered how much Elijah loved to care for the horses.

Soon, Hannah was done with the work and, one by one, led the horses into their stables. She finished up, put the lock on the stable doors, and then began walking towards the house.

Becca and the boys were in the kitchen cleaning and putting the dishes away after the night's supper.

"The barn needs fixing," Hannah repeated, this time not in her thoughts but loud enough for Becca to hear. "That place is a disaster waiting to happen. Becca, would you please remind me tomorrow to inform Mr. Nathaniel about the work that needs to be done there?"

"Okay, sister," Becca responded.

Hannah joined the kids in clearing the kitchen while they talked about their day's activities. When they were done, they went to the family room to chat before retiring to bed.

"Sister, have you heard the news?" Becca inquired.

"What news?" Hannah asked.

Her sister stared at her wide-eyed for a few seconds before opening up.

"I heard some rumors. I don't know how true it is, but... erm, I heard that Amos is back in town."

Hannah was dazed.

"Where did you hear that from?" Hannah queried.

"From some of my friends. At first, they didn't know who he was as they thought him strange. He has changed, sister. But in many ways, they say it seems for the better."

Hannah did not say any more, but she was greatly troubled.

Sensing the uneasiness and worry on her face, her sister suggested she retire for the night. "I think you should get some rest. I'll help Jeremiah with his study while you go lie down in the room."

"Alright. Thank you, Becca. You do so much for us," Hannah replied soberly as she put down the books and went to bed.

Hannah lay in bed restless, unable to close her eyes. So many thoughts raced through her mind. Amos was back in town. She wasn't even sure if it was true, but the news greatly distressed her.

What if they crossed paths? How would she react? What would she say? Did she even need to say anything?

Then, she cautioned herself. She was unduly working herself up. It's been eight years. He probably doesn't remember her, nor would he care about her anyway. He was probably married with children by now.

What was he even doing back in town?

Hannah rolled from one side of the bed to another, unable to sleep.

After Becca was done with the lessons, she put the boys in bed and tucked them in, then went to Hannah's room to check on her. She knocked lightly on the door to ascertain if Hannah was still awake. When she heard nothing, she pushed the door as quietly as possible and tiptoed in.

Hannah pretended to be asleep because she feared her sister seeing her in such a miserable state. Becca slowly pulled the covering over her shoulders, kissed her lightly on her forehead, and whispered goodnight.

Hannah couldn't help herself as she got teary-eyed thinking about how much her sister cared about her and the children. Since their mom died, shortly after their father had, Becca, although younger, had provided more moral support for Hannah than she could ever ask for. She was there for all of them at her own expense, often missing activities with friends to tend to her, the bakery, the boys, and the barn. She needed to find a way to relieve Becca so she could have the time to experience life as a teenager, just like she was privileged to.

With these distracting thoughts, Hannah forgot about Amos and his return and soon fell into a sound slumber.

The following day, Hannah woke up quite early to do the chores around the house and prepare breakfast for the family. She was going to give Becca a treat today and time off alone to seek her pastime. So, before the rest of the family woke, she had finished breakfast and was about to set the table. They exchanged greetings warmly as they always did every morning. The boys helped out with setting the table, and Hannah dished out the meals, serving everyone as they took their seats.

"You know what, Becca?" Hannah asked cheerfully, in between munching a spoonful of the honeyed pancake she had made.

"What?" Becca smiled, a little confused at the bustle of energy her sister carried this morning.

"You should take the day off," she announced. "Go out, meet up with your friends, do something for fun, will you?"

"Hmm! That doesn't sound bad at all," Becca laughed. "But are you sure you can get through the day with little Noah at the bakery with you? I don't mind taking him along with me."

"No. We'll be fine. There's not much to be done at the bakery today anyways."

"Fine. I'll take the day off. Thank you, sis."

"You're welcome."

They ate the rest of the meal, chattering about their expectations for the day. Noah was the most excited to be spending the day by his mother's side, where he gets to taste some of her delicious pastries right off the oven.

<h2 style="text-align:center">Chapter Six</h2>

The bakery was a little slow today. The number of walk-ins was quite small, which was common in the afternoons. More people come in the mornings to get breakfast and afternoon lunch. Noah was napping after stuffing himself with more pies than he could manage, and Hannah lay him on the makeshift bed behind the counter.

Hannah sat on one of the stools behind the counter, reviewing the inventory and balancing her accounts. The bell dinged, and as she looked up, she saw Mary walk into the bakery. Closing her books, she got up and received her friend in a warm embrace. After exchanging pleasantries, they took seats opposite each other.

"How are you today?" Hannah asked.

"I'm fine, and you?"

"I'm fine. You look quite exhausted. How about some tea and something to eat?"

"Oh dear, don't bother. Thank you for offering, Hannah. You take care of everyone so well," Mary said.

"Oh! Think nothing of it. You're my best friend, and you're eating some of my delicious whoopie pie," she insisted as she got up, cut a slice into a saucer, and made some mint tea. When she returned, she placed them on the table. "Now, eat that pie and tell me what you think."

Mary picked the fork up and cut a piece. She chewed it slowly, taking time to dissolve the flavors in her mouth, and then she nodded proudly.

"You outdo yourself every time, Hannah. This is delicious. Hmm!" she moaned softly.

The two women laughed loudly as Mary continued work on the pie. When she was done, she wiped her mouth with the cloth napkin and let out a sigh.

"Hannah, I need to tell you something," she began.

Hannah listened raptly. "Is there a problem?" she asked as she reached for her friend's hands.

"No. Yes. Not really. Oh, I don't know how to say it."

Hannah peered at her, visibly confused.

"Amos is back," she finally blurted out.

Hannah's heartbeat quickened as she immediately remembered Becca telling her last night. Still, she managed to maintain her composure and pretended like she was oblivious.

"Oh! He - is?" she stammered, trying not to expose her secret.

Mary nodded in response.

"When?" she inquired, her face already reddening up. She was at a loss at how to behave.

"It's almost a week now, Hannah. He's staying at our home. Based on the history you both share and the fact that you're my best friend, I needed to inform you firsthand in case you stumble upon him in town. I think he's back for good. He seems to have gotten the experiences he needed, and is now ready to come home."

"I really appreciate you informing me, but it's all in the past now. We were young then. There's so much water under the bridge," she laughed nervously. But although Hannah tried not to show too much interest in the topic, she was curious to know about his marital status. "Did he come with his family?" she quizzed.

"No... No, he never got married. And if I'm not mistaken, he might still be in love with you. My husband won't tell me much, but I have heard your name once or twice in passing," she responded knowingly.

Hannah shrugged and got up to clear the table, trying to steer the conversation away from Amos. When she returned, they talked about other things until it was time for Hannah to start tomorrow's breads. Mary got up to leave, and Hannah walked her to the street. The two ladies hugged each other and said their goodbyes.

Deep down, Hannah felt oddly excited to learn that Amos was still single and available. Even though she was not considering remarriage herself, it had been a long time since she last had male company. A few widowers had tried to seek her attention, but she was never really interested in starting a relationship after all that she had been through. She preferred to devote her attention to caring for her young boys, but she would have to agree that the boys could use a male authority in their lives. They needed it.

Noah, who was still an infant when their father passed, did not fully comprehend why he didn't have a father like the other kids they associated with. One time, after

Hannah had tried to explain that their father had gone to be with God, the little boy looked her in the eyes and innocently asked when he would return home. Hannah had been unable to control the tears that streamed down her face as she watched him in his innocence, sighing that his father was taking too long with God.

They had little around the house to remind them of him. All that was left were the shoes and clothes he left behind, which Hannah was too unwilling to give away for fear that they would lose all remembrances of him.

Hannah was proud of her boys. They were very well-mannered, as they should be. However, raising them as a single parent had been quite a challenge. Although everyone in the community invested in their growth, the bulk of the work rested on her shoulders, and she carried on diligently.

By the time Hannah returned from work that evening, she had forgotten to inform Nathaniel about the barn renovation. Or perhaps she was worried she might come across Amos at their home. She needed to avoid being the first one to cross his path.

"Becca," she called out when she got into the house, "I guess I'm not the only one who forgot about informing Nathaniel to come fix the fence," she accused, suddenly remembering her own task.

"I'm sorry, sis. It had slipped my mind in the morning, but when I remembered while I was out, I had gone to meet him myself at his shed and notified him."

"That's good!" Hannah sighed in relief. Now she would not have to worry about meeting with Amos anytime soon. "Did you see him?" she asked Becca impulsively.

"Who?"

"Amos. Did you see him while you were over there?"

"No. I didn't," Becca replied, looking at her sister curiously.

Hannah asked how her day went, realizing she needed to change the subject.

"I went on a nice walk to gather some apples, then took care of some mending that needing doing. I also thought of a new recipe for apple butter."

Hannah smiled. "You had a good day indeed. I hope you can also make time to go to the Sing? You need to find someone you may want to court and spend more time with people your age."

"Well, maybe now that Amos is in town, you two may get to pick up from where you stopped. You need a relationship yourself,"

Hannah eyed her wordlessly.

"But I mean it, sister Hannah. What if he came back for you?"

"That is a big 'what if.' So you don't think that he may be married?" Hannah asked, although she already knew the answer to that.

"Well, there was no mention of a wife or children. So I'm pretty sure he's still unmarried."

"Or maybe his family is where he left them," Hannah chipped in, teasing her sister gently.

Becca surrendered. "Okay, you win!" She put her hands up in the air as she moved away to fold the clean laundry sitting in a basket on the table.

Chapter Seven

Amos did not join Nathaniel at the woodshed that day, so he wasn't aware that Hannah's sister had visited. When Nathaniel returned to the house, he found Amos at the small shed he often worked at whenever he worked from home, shaving some wood.

"Hey, Amos," he called at him.

Amos looked up from his shavings and welcomed him back. The two men shook hands.

"How was work today?"

"It was fine. I was able to finish and deliver a set of stools," Nathaniel said.

"Good, then. Tomorrow we'll work together at the shed. I thought I'd be able to muster up the courage to go see Hannah at her bakery, but I was not able to get past the door. It's depressing."

"Well, you're in luck. We'll be working on Hannah's stable tomorrow. Her sister came around today and solicited my help with their broken fence. So by evening tomorrow, we'll head over there to inspect the damage and take some measurements," Nathaniel said.

Amos got up; he was suddenly feeling hot. He paced around the shed.

"Does she know I'm here in town?"

"I don't know, but this is a small community, and word gets around fast. I'm fairly sure that she may have heard by now."

He was still anxious about seeing her for the first time in eight years. He didn't know what to expect. This was his mess, and there was no escaping it. It had to be fixed.

Around four the following evening, the two men rode their buggy down to Hannah's house. When they got to the drive, Amos stayed back while Nathaniel walked up to the front porch and knocked on the door. He heard footsteps approaching, then the door opened.

"Good evening, Nathaniel. Welcome to our home."

"Thank you, Becca. Good evening. I suppose Hannah is not yet back, is she?" he asked.

"No, sir. She isn't, but it's sundown already. She'll be back shortly. Would you like to wait for her to return first?"

Nathaniel nodded at the girl. "Oh! Yes, we will, but before she returns, I'd like to take a look around to see what we may need for the repairs. First, you'll have to show us around the back."

"Us? You're not alone?" Becca asked as she squinted her eyes to see who was in the buggy. "Is that Amos?" she whispered when she could not get his features.

Nathaniel smiled knowingly. "Yes, it is."

Becca excused herself and went back into the house to find some footwear. By the time she returned, Amos was out of the buggy and standing next to Nathaniel.

"How are the boys?" Nathaniel asked when she stepped out of the door.

"Oh, they're very well. They're tending to their chores right now."

Becca led the way while the two men followed behind. They walked to the back of the house where the stable was.

"Here," Becca said as she pointed to the side of the fence that was falling apart.

Nathaniel stepped forward and inspected the damage, then took some measurements. From the look of things, the fence needed to be torn down and rebuilt. The wood was rotting, not only from the wet weather but also from insect infestation.

The men waited for Hannah, but it was taking too long, so they left a message with Becca and promised to come back the next evening to start the work. When Hannah finally returned, Becca was waiting at the door eagerly to tell her that Amos had visited their home.

"Welcome back, sis," she greeted as she pulled Hannah quickly into the house. "Amos came around today. He came with Nathaniel. Well, they came to check the work for the barn, of course, but..." She narrated every detail, from the time she found the two men in the driveway to the time they left without missing a beat. By the time she was done, Hannah's face was flustered.

"Did he say anything?"

"Who? Nathaniel?"

"No. Amos"

"Oh! He was quiet most of the time. He was simply following Nathaniel's cues, but he kept glancing at the driveway as if he were expecting you to return," she said, batting her eyes at her sister.

"Oh, go away, you silly child," Hannah laughed, jokingly pushing her away.

"They'll be back tomorrow to start the work, though," Becca finally announced.

***

The next evening, the two men arrived and were tearing down the fence in preparation for the work. A few minutes after, a buggy made a stop outside the house. Hannah stepped out of the carriage and started to make her way toward the house. She noticed the buggy sitting in her driveway and knew that Nathaniel and Amos were around.

Hannah tried as much as she could to put on a brave face, but she could feel her heart beating at a faster rate. She quickened her steps as she drew closer, but just before she could step onto the porch, Amos appeared, heading over to their buggy to pick some tools. The two froze when their eyes met, and they stared at each other for a confusing moment.

"Hello, Hannah," Amos greeted when he finally found his voice.

"Hello," Hannah muttered under her breath as she quickly stepped into the house and closed the door behind her.

Amos stood there for a few seconds trying to process what had just happened, then he shrugged and continued toward the back of the carriage. Reaching in, he picked up the tools and started back towards the stable.

Inside, Hannah paced the room, her lips quivering and body trembling. She felt a wild mix of emotions. She knew they were going to meet somehow. What she didn't know was how she would feel. All of a sudden, the emotions she had felt the night she found out that Amos had left town resurged, and a combination of anger and excitement rushed through her bones. He was so kind, and so handsome. She couldn't stay mad at that, could she? She resented him, yet she felt some strange kind of warm feeling for him.

She hadn't felt this way in a long time and wasn't sure if that was good or bad.

Slowly, Hannah moved to the window and watched them from behind the curtain. She could see the two men conversing in hushed tones. She strained her ears in hopes that she could hear a bit of their conversation. She imagined Amos telling Nathaniel how she had just made a fool of herself before him, and her cheeks began to flush again.

The barn fence had been brought down completely, and Amos and Nathaniel were sorting out the wood suitable for reuse.

"I ran into Hannah just as she was about to step into the house."

Nathaniel looked up at him. "And?"

"Well, I could only manage a 'Hello.' But before I could say anything else, she had dashed into the house, closing the door behind her."

Nathaniel smiled as he bent over and picked some wood. "Well, not bad for a first time. You'll do better next time. You just need to have patience."

The men continued the rest of the work in silence. When it was getting late, they decided to stop to continue the next day.

Becca offered them a basket of home-baked pies, which they happily accepted.

That night, Hannah lay in bed replaying their encounter on the porch over and over in her head. She wondered why she had behaved so strangely. She should be mad at him, so why did she feel she wanted to see him again? How did he still manage such a hold on her eight years later despite what he had done?

Chapter Eight

Throughout the week, Nathaniel and Amos worked on the fence. A few times, Amos would stay behind to clean the stables, stack fresh hay for the horses, and change their water. Unfortunately, he still didn't get a chance to speak with Hannah as she avoided him altogether, even though she had come out once or twice to see the work. She would intentionally not look his way or pretend he wasn't there.

Hannah's boys, however, were taken to Amos. Whenever they were at home while the men were working, they would hover around the yard. They always ask him to stay behind and play with them or teach them a new trick. Amos loved to indulge them and would go on horseback rides with them or hunt insects together on the grass. The children adored him, and even the horses soon got used to him, braying softly whenever he walked into the stables.

One evening, Amos was determined to make a move and set things straight with Hannah. He needed to stop being such a coward. So, after Hannah had returned and settled in, he walked up to the door and knocked. It took what felt like forever before the bolts unlatch. Finally, Amos looked up and found himself staring into her deep-green eyes. He felt a knot tighten in his stomach.

Swallowing a lump, he stammered, "May - may I get a cup of water, please?"

Hannah only nodded in response, retreated into the room, and returned with a cup.

Their hands brushed against each other in that instant, and Hannah felt a flush rise to her cheeks. She turned to hurry back into the house when Amos caught her hand.

"Please," he pleaded.

Hannah turned red.

"Please wait, I know," he stuttered. "I know I'm such a fool. I was young and foolish, but I'd give anything to turn things around. But, please, Hannah, let's talk. There's so much to be said." He looked at her with pleading eyes.

Suddenly, she was sixteen again. Her eyes flashed with tears, which she fought to hold back. There was a tightness in her chest, and she seemed to have lost her voice.

"Please, Hannah."

Slowly, she nodded and closed the door behind her.

"First, I need to apologize for leaving the way I did. It was very unfair. You know, I always felt like I didn't belong here. There was something in me that always felt unsettled, unalive then. But now I realize it was just a juvenile fantasy getting the best of me. Yes, the city had more opportunities, and I took advantage of them. I never betrayed our faith, but I did profit in both knowledge and money from the Englisher world. Maybe more than I would have made around here. Still, I never found that peace I yearned for, that sense of belonging," he finished abashedly after they had sat on the bench. There was silence between them. He hoped Hannah would say something.

"So why are you telling me this now?" she demanded, trying to be unmoved by his speech.

"You deserved to know my decision then. I know it's a little too late now, but I wanted to try to make things right," he said.

Moments passed before Amos spoke again, standing now.

"Nathaniel told me what happened to your husband. I'm so sorry about that too."

Hannah felt a bit of sadness sting her throat, and her eyes grew misty.

"Thank you," she managed. "So, why did you decide to come home?" she finally inquired against her better judgment as the urge kept gnawing at her.

Amos hesitated, then began, "Well, I got what I wanted, but I missed more than I expected."

She nodded and felt herself relax. "I need to go get some sleep now," Hannah finally announced. "There's a lot of work to be done at the bakery tomorrow."

"That reminds me. I hope you don't mind me coming around to work on the barn," he smiled.

"Not at all. I don't mind. I enjoy the extra hand. Thank you. And oh! The boys seem to enjoy you coming around," Hannah said, smiling.

"Your boys are so sweet and so smart. And Noah, he never wants to let go," he said, laughing.

"Yes. He was quite young when his father passed, so he tends to look up to every male figure as a father," she said soberly.

"Well, I will take my leave. I'll see you tomorrow when I return."

"Good night, Amos Miller."

"Good night, Hannah," he said as he walked off the porch and mounted his horse strapped by the barn fence.

She watched him as his horse trotted out of the compound. Then, she gently closed the door and retired to bed when they were both out of sight.

***

Amos had adjusted back to the more conservative lifestyle of his old community. He wore loose-fitting black trousers and blue shirts with his suspenders. He was also associating more with the villagers and forming bonds of friendship and strong connections.

For the next few weeks, Amos came to the house in the mornings or evenings to care for the horses and stables. He would spend time with the boys, helping them with schoolwork and teaching them the basics of cleaning the stables, feeding, and caring for the horses.

Hannah was happy to see him each evening when she returned from work. Amos, too, would dally around sometimes even when he had finished the chores and there was nothing left to do. They would often sit together on the porch, reminiscing and sharing their hopes for the future. Sometimes Hannah would join him at the stables, or they would tend to the garden together. Hannah would save him some of her best pies and pastries and would often ask him to try her new recipes before she introduced them.

One evening, while they took a stroll along the country road after a horse ride, Amos expressed his feelings for Hannah. He confessed never stopped thinking about her, and asked that they continue their long-paused courtship.

Hannah had asked for time to consider the proposal.

Chapter Nine

One early December morning, after Hannah had left for the bakery, Becca stepped out of the house to get some material from a neighbor's house. The boys were home, getting ready to clean the stables after doing their homework. It was a typical day, to all accounts.

But on this day, for reasons unknown, a still smoldering bit of ember tumbled silently from last night's fire out of the fireplace, where it settled on the floor rug. Before long, a fire had started, and smoke began to build.

Fortunately, Amos had driven down to the house to assist in the stable like he did every day when he caught sight of the flames in the window. He ran into the house immediately, breaking down the front door. Once inside, he heard the boys, now aware of the situation as the air in the home got choked, screaming frantically as they tried to put out the fire. Amos rushed in and hurried them outside to safety. Thankfully, the boys were unhurt.

By now, the neighbors were alarmed and gathered round to salvage whatever they could. The horses were quickly released from their stalls. After delivering the boys to Becca, Amos ran back into the house, hoping to find anything of value he could save. He quickly picked a basket and threw a few things in before running back out as the fire began to rage.

By the time the fire service arrived, the house was almost razed down to the ground before the fire was finally put out.

When news of the fire got to Hannah, it had taken all of her strength to remain calm.

"Hannah, the boys are safe," one of them assured her. "They had been pulled out of the house by Amos Miller, who had arrived on time."

When they got to the house, a crowd of community members and a fire service department crew were outside what used to be their home. Hannah could not control her tears. She was utterly devastated at her loss and relieved her children were safe. She rushed to her boys and scooped them in a tight embrace.

Hannah turned around and searched for Amos. His buggy was standing outside, but he was nowhere to be found.

"Where's Amos?" Hannah asked as she ran back towards Becca. "Where's Amos?" She repeated.

"He's inside the ambulance."

"What?"

She didn't wait for an answer as she ran back to the ambulance. She had seen it on the street but had not realized anyone was inside.

"Amos Miller, where is he?"

The man showed Hannah inside the ambulance, where Amos lay on a stretcher being attended to by some paramedics.

"What happened to him?"

"He suffered mild asphyxia."

Hannah looked at the paramedic, and sensing her confusion, he explained to her that Amos had passed out due to smoke inhalation while he was saving the boys.

Had the boys remained inside the house much longer than they did, they would have been knocked unconscious too.

Hannah rode to the town hospital, since the paramedics needed to take Amos to the doctors there. They also thought getting the boys checked out would be a good idea.

Chapter Ten

The boys were soon discharged from the hospital and returned home to Becca. Hannah had to stay back with Amos as he was still unconscious. He had gotten some burns on his leg that were not obvious before, and he had been treated and bandaged.

Hannah was worried sick. She had previously lost someone she loved and was unwilling to lose another. Looking down as he slept, she prayed fervently for his safe recovery.

"Please, Gott, help him heal. I love him, and I do not want to lose him again."

That evening, Amos was awake and doing much better. The doctors said that he would be well enough the next day to come home.

"Hey," he said after the doctors had given him the news.

Hannah smiled up at him.

"Hey."

"How are the boys?" he asked.

"They're fine. They were here too but left. Amos, you saved their lives. You saved my boys' lives. I can never thank you enough for this. Thank you," she said while holding on to his hands.

Amos nodded and mouthed, "You're welcome."

"I'm just glad I showed up at the right moment."

Later that night, after the doctors had made their ward rounds, Hannah sat curled up on a chair beside the bed, knitting a sweater.

"So, did you mean those words you said?" Amos asked.

"What?" Hannah asked, looking up at him.

He bore a serious look on his face.

"Those words you said while I was out."

"What words?" she insisted, feigning ignorance.

"That you loved me?" he questioned, turning himself gently onto his side.

Hannah smiled, and he said nothing more. Soon, he dozed off, and Hannah pulled up the sheets and tucked him in.

The next day, they were discharged and ready to return home. Nathaniel and some elders came over in their horse-drawn buggies, and Amos was wheeled out to the carriage. He was cleared to go but would need to use a cane around for a while.

As they approached what used to be Hannah's home, a two-story wood frame house stood in its place. Hannah could not believe her eyes. She knew that her house would be rebuilt, as was the custom in their close-knit community, but she never knew it would surpass her imagination.

Hannah was dropped off at home while Amos was taken to Nathaniel's home, where he would recuperate. Hannah promised to visit them later.

Becca, Jeremiah, and Noah were so happy to have Hannah back home. They showed Hannah the considerable supply of donations that kept coming in. They'd not had to cook ever since that day. Hannah was filled with appreciation and promised to write thank you notes to their donors later.

***

It had been a week since the fire incident, and life was slowly bearing a semblance of normalcy. Hannah had resumed work at the bakery. Jeremiah had continued school, and Becca still cared for Noah while completing chores at the house and sometimes helping out at the bakery. The four of them would work on the stables early at sunrise and sunset as they used to before Amos came into their lives.

That afternoon, there was a knock on the door.

"Well, hello," Hannah chirped. "I was hoping you'd come by soon." She looked lovely, and Amos felt a warmth spread through his chest.

He smiled at her and held out an object wrapped in cloth. "I think this is yours, Hannah."

"What is this?" she asked, looking curious.

"That day of the fire, after rescuing the boys, I ran back inside the house to find anything of value I could save. It's not much, but it's all I could gather before the smoke worsened."

"Oh my!" Hannah gasped as she uncovered the lovely porcelain dish. It was the very one Elijah had proposed to her with.

"Thank you. Thank you so much," she said through misty eyes.

Amos took her hand in his. "I love you, Hannah," he said seriously. "And I would like the chance to redeem myself to you, if you will have me. If you would allow me to court you, that is."

Hannah nodded with a grin. "I will have you, Amos. I had a good life with Elijah, and I loved him. But I love you too, and I know now the heart can hold more than we ever imagined."

Amos smiled, and together they went to find the boys and tell them the good news.

The End

FREE GIFT

Just to say thanks for checking our works we like to gift you

Our Exclusive Never Before Released Books

100% FREE!

Please GO TO

http://cleanromancepublishing.com/gift

And get your FREE gift

Thanks for being such a wonderful client.

Please Check out My Other Works

By checking out the link below

http://cleanromancepublishing.com/rbauth

Thank You

Many thanks for taking the time to buy and read through this book.

It means lots to be supported by SPECIAL readers like YOU.

Hope you enjoyed the book; please support my writing by leaving an honest review to assist other readers.

.

With Regards,

Ruth Bawell